What Is a Migrant?

A FELIPE ADVENTURE STORY

What Is a Migrant?

Florance W. Taylor

Pictures by George Overlie

Lerner Publications Company

Minneapolis, Minnesota

With gratitude to the canning company offi-
cials involved, the Migrant Council, and the
public schools, especially to Mr. W.E. Schellhardt, Mr. N.E. Duchette, Mr. Leland Berg-
strom, Mrs. Mary Messner, Mrs. Dorothy
Whitehouse, and Mrs. Helen Kaufman.

International Standard Book Number: 0-8225-0142-2
Library of Congress Catalog Card Number: 72-165316

To Mr. W. E. Schellhardt

Felipe Fuentes was all scrubbed and shining, ready for school. He and his family had arrived in Illinois just last night, after a long trip from Texas riding in the back of a truck. The Fuentes were migrant farm workers. They had come, with several other families, to work in the town of Lockton. Mama and Papa Fuentes would spend all day picking vegetables in the fields. But ten-year-old Felipe would not be working. He would be in school.

"Come on," called Carlos, one of Felipe's friends. "It's time to go." Carlos was two years older than Felipe, and he had been in Lockton the summer before. He was rounding up all the new children in the migrant camp to take them across town to the school.

As they walked through the camp, Felipe saw that it was much larger than he had thought. There were many buildings for the workers, as well as a big canning factory. Each large building held a number of migrant families.

"Carlos, how many people live here?" Felipe asked.

"I don't know," Carlos replied. "Several truckloads came here before we did. Papa said there were 450 people last year."

"Well, I guess there are lots of families here from Texas," Felipe said.

As they came close to the big building next to the railroad track, Felipe heard a clanging, chugging noise.

"What's that, Carlos?" he asked.

"The canning factory," Carlos told him. "I think they're canning asparagus now. The company ships canned vegetables all over the United States. But we can't go in that building."

"I see why it's so near the railroad track," Felipe said. "The company must ship the cans in freight cars."

"Sure," Carlos replied.

MEADE PARK ELEMENTARY SCHOOL
LEARNING CENTER

Suddenly Carlos snapped his fingers. "We didn't bring our report cards."

"Report cards?" Felipe was surprised. "What would we do with them?"

"The principal will want them for proof of the grade we were in down in Texas." Carlos shrugged. "Well, we didn't know that we were leaving that night until after school. So we just couldn't get the cards."

Carlos led the children right to the principal's office.

"Here we are again, Miss Miller," he said to the tall, gray-haired woman sitting behind the desk.

Miss Miller smiled. "It's good to see you, Carlos. We've been expecting you. I see you've brought us some new boys and girls."

"Yes'm."

The principal turned to the children and asked, "Did you bring your report cards?"

Felipe looked at Carlos and waited for him to speak.

"No, Miss Miller, we didn't have time to get them," Carlos explained.

Miss Miller frowned a little. "Tell me what grade you were in at your Texas school. We'll try you in the same one here. Carlos, you were in the fifth grade, I believe."

"Yes'm. But I'm in the sixth now."

"I'm sure you know where the sixth grade room is," the principal said. "You may try it there for a week. Then we'll see."

After Carlos left, Miss Miller asked, "Who is in the fifth grade?"

Felipe raised his hand.

"Your name, please," said Miss Miller.

"Felipe Fuentes."

"Report to Mrs. Sands, Felipe. Her room is at the top of the stairway on the second floor."

In the fifth grade classroom, the children were busy taking an arithmetic test. Some of them smiled at Felipe and then went on with their work.

"We're glad to have you with us, Felipe," Mrs. Sands said. "Will you try our arithmetic test?"

Felipe drew a deep breath and nodded. This school seemed like the one in Texas. He began to work the problems.

The first day of school did not go too badly for Felipe. And that evening Mama and Papa were in high spirits after their first day of work. Mama did not even complain about the cold weather. She smiled as she said, "We cut asparagus today, lots of it." She spoke to the family in Spanish. The Fuentes were Texans, but Mama and Papa spoke only Spanish. Felipe had learned English at school and, like the other migrant children, knew both languages. Mama continued, "We can't take Roberto, Juanito, or little Luis to the fields anymore. It's not allowed."

Felipe's heart sank. "Will I have to stay home and take care of them?" he asked.

Mama's eyes twinkled. "No, Felipe. You go to school and work hard. Mrs. Alvarez will look after Luis. She is not able to go to the fields yet."

"What about Roberto and Juanito?" Felipe still looked worried.

Papa smiled. "You see, they do things for us here in Illinois. A young lady comes to our camp each morning to play with our little children. 'Supervised playing' they call it."

Felipe brightened. "Then I can go back to school tomorrow?"

"Of course," Mama replied. Then she added, "We will make more money in the fields without the three boys. If we don't have to watch them, we can work faster."

During the next few days Felipe did quite well in school—that is, until he did something on the playground, something that later made him feel ashamed.

One morning he saw a new girl in the fourth grade line. She was standing just across from him. He stared and stared. Was this a little girl or an angel? Her skin was very fair, and she wore her cream-colored hair in a ponytail. Her blue dress was topped with a sweater that matched her hair.

Felipe thought of the spun sugar candies his mother always made for their special feast day on November 2, the Day of the Dead. That ponytail looked like strands of spun sugar.

The little girl suddenly turned around and caught Felipe staring at her. She screwed up her face and stuck her tongue out. Then she tossed her head and turned away.

Felipe didn't know why he did it, but he reached over and yanked her ponytail hard.

The girl glared at Felipe a second and then screamed, "Ouch! You let my hair alone." Then she pinched his arm.

MEADE PARK ELEMENTARY SCHOOL
LEARNING CENTER

Her scream pierced the quiet of the school ground, and every child turned to see what had happened. Miss Graves, the fourth grade teacher, hurried over and seized Felipe by his arm.

She looked first at him and then at the little girl. "What's the meaning of this?" she asked sharply.

"He pulled my hair, and it hurt," the girl replied.

"Felipe, why did you pull her hair?" asked Miss Graves.

Felipe hung his head and scraped a pebble with his shoe. "I don't know," he replied in a whisper.

Miss Graves then took the little girl by the arm too. "I think both of you had better talk with Miss Miller about this." She marched them past the other children and into the principal's office.

Miss Miller looked at the two children for a few moments. Then she said, "Karen King, are you in trouble the second day you are in school? And Felipe, you've been here only about two weeks. What happened?"

"He pulled my hair," the little girl replied, "and it hurt."

"Why did you pull Karen's hair, Felipe?" asked Miss Miller.

Felipe looked at the principal, his brown eyes troubled. "I guess I just wanted to see if it was real, ma'am. It looks like the spun sugar candy Mama makes for our feast days. I was just looking at her and she stuck her tongue out at me." He didn't mention that Karen had pinched him.

Karen, angry now because Felipe had told on her, said, "Well, he's just a filthy Mexican migrant."

Miss Miller's eyes flashed. But she said quietly, "Sit down, children. Karen, what is a filthy Mexican migrant?"

Karen squirmed in her chair. "I don't know. That's what Grandmother King calls the people who come to work for the canning company. She says that they never should have come to Lockton."

The principal frowned. "Karen, I know your grandmother well. But she is wrong about these people. Look at Felipe."

Karen scowled but looked at Felipe.

"Now, you can see that he isn't filthy," Miss Miller said. "In fact, he's quite clean, Karen. So the word *filthy* does not apply to him." Turning to Felipe, she asked, "Where were you born?"

"In Texas, ma'am. In the Rio Grande Valley," he replied.

"Were your parents born in Texas too?" the principal asked.

"Yes, ma'am."

Miss Miller now turned to Karen. "You see, Felipe is an American, just like you are. It's true his ancestors came from Mexico. I suppose people call the migrants Mexicans because they speak Spanish and look like the people of Mexico. But they are Americans, not Mexicans."

Karen sighed but did not reply.

Miss Miller continued, "Do you know what the word *migrant* means, Karen?"

The little girl shook her head.

"Felipe, do you?" Miss Miller asked.

"No," replied Felipe, "but people up here do call us migrants."

Miss Miller took a dictionary from the shelf behind her desk and said, "Let's see what *migrant* means." When she found the word, she read its meaning aloud: "A migrant is a person who moves from one place to another to work for a time. Sometimes moving with the seasons." She looked at Felipe. "Why did your family come to Lockton?"

"To work in the fields for the Midwest Canning Company," he answered. "Papa said we'd make more money here and live better. And we do."

Miss Miller smiled for the first time since the children had come to the office. "And you'll go home to Texas when the summer is over. Karen, why did you leave your home in St. Louis and come here to stay with your grandmother?"

Karen brightened. "Because my parents went to Central America to do some work for the University."

Felipe looked at Karen with sympathy. He wouldn't want to stay in Texas without his parents. Not even with his grandmother.

"Why didn't you go with your parents, Karen?" asked Miss Miller.

"Mother was afraid I might get sick," Karen answered. "She heard that the malaria is bad down there."

"You'll be here about six months, your grandmother told me," said Miss Miller. "That's about as long as Felipe will be here. In a way, you are a migrant too, Karen. And so are your parents."

Karen looked puzzled. "But Miss Miller, my father is a professor. He's doing important work in Central America."

"I'm sure he is," Miss Miller replied. "Felipe's parents are doing important work here too."

"I don't understand how working in the fields is important," Karen said.

Miss Miller spoke up quickly. "Any honest work is important, Karen. I remember that your father worked in the fields here to earn his way through college."

"I know," Karen replied. "And Grandmother says the migrants take the work away from our people."

Miss Miller frowned and said sharply, "Your grandmother knows we don't have people here anymore to do the field work."

"What happened to them?" Karen asked.

"Stooping in the fields day after day is hard work," Miss Miller explained. "The old farmhands left because they could get easier jobs elsewhere. So the canning company brings families from Texas. Without these workers, the farm owners couldn't raise enough vegetables to make a living."

Karen nodded her head. "Then the owners wouldn't get any money from their farms."

"That's right, Karen," the principal agreed. "And the women couldn't afford to buy dresses from your grandmother each season. Remind her of that."

Felipe looked at Miss Miller and said, "I'm sorry I pulled Karen's hair."

The principal replied, "I'm sure you are, Felipe. I hope you two will be good friends and set an example of friendship for the other children."

Felipe grinned at Karen. "I'll try to make it up to you. For pulling your hair, I mean."

"Okay, Felipe," she replied. "And I'll try to make it up to you for saying what I did. I'm really sorry."

Miss Miller walked with the two children to the door of her office. "Go back to your rooms now," she said. "And I'm sure you won't be sent to my office again."

At home that evening Felipe didn't have the courage to tell his parents about his trouble at school. But he knew it was all right, now that he and Karen were friends. Besides, Mama and Papa were bursting with news of the shopping trip. Papa had gone to town and bought popcorn, candy, a new stroller for eighteen-month-old Luis, and some summer blankets for all of them.

After dinner, as everyone was eating popcorn and talking and laughing, Felipe sat silently, smiling to himself. He was thinking how happy he was to live in Illinois, to be in school, and to have a new friend.

Felipe
Adventure Stories

From Texas to Illinois

What Is a Migrant?

Ball Two!

The School Picnic

Where's Luis?

The Corn Festival

A Plane Ride

We specialize in producing quality books for young people. For a complete list please write

 Lerner Publications Company
241 First Avenue North, Minneapolis, Minnesota 55401